Seasonal Rights

Books by Daniel Halpern

Seasonal Rights

POEMS BY

Daniel Halpern

The Viking Press / New York

Penguin Books

PS
3558
.A397
S4

Penguin Books Ltd, Harmondsworth, Middlesex, England
Penguin Books, 625 Madison Avenue, New York,
New York 10022, U.S.A. '
Penguin Books Australia Ltd, Ringwood, Victoria, Australia
Penguin Books Canada Limited, 2801 John Street,
Markham, Ontario, Canada L3R 1B4
Penguin Books (N.Z.) Ltd, 182–190 Wairau Road,
Auckland 10, New Zealand
First published in 1982 in simultaneous hardcover and paperback
editions by The Viking Press and Penguin Books,
625 Madison Avenue, New York, New York 10022
Published simultaneously in Canada
Copyright © 1979, 1980, 1981, 1982 by Daniel Halpern
All rights reserved
Library of Congress Cataloging in Publication Data
Halpern, Daniel, 1945– / Seasonal rights.
  I. Title.
PS3558.A397S4   811'.54   82–70126
ISBN 0–670–62731–3 (hardbound)   AACR2
ISBN 0 14 042.304 4 (paperbound)
Printed in the United States of America
Set in Linotype Electra

ACKNOWLEDGMENTS

Grateful acknowledgment is made to the following magazines in which
most of these poems originally appeared: *American Poetry Review*:
"The Hermit," "Leaving Summer"; *Antioch Review*: "The Last
Days of the Year"; *Esquire*: "How to Eat Alone"; *Georgia Review*:
"This Place"; *Grand Street*: "Trees in Various Climates"; *Harper's
Magazine*: "Portoncini dei Morti"; *Iowa Review*: "Elegies for
Careless Love," "Dead Fish," and "Under Darkness"; *The Missouri
Review*: "For Cats" and "Night Food"; *The Nation*: "Birthright"
and "Driving"; *New England Review*: "Snapshot of Hué" and "The
Dwelling Air"; *New Republic*: "Spend"; *The New Yorker*: "The
Corpse of the Insensitive," "Return, Starting Out," "This Time of the
Year," and "White Field"; *Ohio Review*: "Nude" and "Calling
West"; *The Paris Review*: "Passing"; *Poetry*: "Late," "The End of
Vigil," "Return," "The Storm," and "Summer Constellations";
Poetry Now: "The Romance" (under the title "Beginning Status Quo
Final Scene"); *Seattle Review*: "Lights in the Dark" and "Water";
Virginia Quarterly Review: "Night Scene" and "Sunday Avenue";
Water Table: "No Letters."

for Jeanne

Contents

I

II

I

White Field

It is like standing beyond
a snowfield with a single
set of footprints across it
and you say, Those prints are mine,
because no one else has ever been here.
All day the snow comes down,
all day you tell yourself what you feel,
but you remain in that place
beyond the snowfield.
Is there better proof
of your presence than
this open field, where you stand
now looking back across the white
expanse that is once more new to you?
As snow fills the places
where you must have walked,
you start back to where you began,
that place you again prepare to leave,
alone and warm, again intact, starting out.

The Corpse of the Insensitive

The mountainside or pasture hills
are gauzy green and a few cows
sleep on the ground—a sign of rain
someone who doesn't know says. With tongues

the cows graze the body in the grass.

The woodsmoke from the house is soaked with rain,
the rain continues, low clouds,
wind, a chill and so on.
Yet we stand on the crossbeam redwood patio

and discuss the body in the grass.

It has been summer here and now it's fall.
No one is ready to begin the climb into winter.
Nothing in government has been settled
although a strike in Poland is over.
The moon spins in a socket, the young touch

through the filament clothes of the body in the grass.

End-of-the-season, turn-of-the-leaves,
so much left behind: summer pets, touch
and one or two small things said once
and never said again, or remembered

after addressing the body in the grass.

We rise in the first snow of winter
on the heat of woodfire,
our bodies partly spent in summer's slow decomposition.
We rise up on our own heat, simultaneous,

as if that body rising in the grass were ours.

Water

On the edge of the sea you ask certain questions
and listen for the answers to come back
like the tide, like the cycles of men
and women in their temperaments.

These are words that swim back
to tell us what that sound was,
what that light to the north was,
what family of bird held that long, high

note. That is why we are standing
here, at night, and why
we are given
sound and the chance to see.

That is why what is out there at night
must remain mysterious for so long—
night being to those standing and asking
endless and religious—and why the body

of water must be there to carry away
what collapses around us.
It is why the mysterious
can give itself over to make valuable

what is simple, to make simple
the valuable never quite with us,
so that out of the darkness over water
the new day with nothing known can begin.

Of the Air

Tonight, in the country, I stood awhile
under the dying oaks—the caterpillars
eat everything but stone—and one by one
starlings flung themselves at me
from the trees, pulling up
at the last moment and sweeping back
into the ornamentally fading sky.
At first I thought they were simply
playful, but they got closer and closer,
their whistling shrill.

If just one bird flew with intent into the window,
shattering the glass, I could believe
that there is something of substance
in their lives, but their bones are hollow—
I imagine that
without marrow they can't suffer,
that misery won't exist in air:
once torn from the earth
it is lifted up and dispersed.

It is still light out and I return
to prepare dinner. I have
something sorrowful keeping me here.

Somewhere there are people beginning
to make fires. Their lives,
of earthly marrow, work the fields.
At night, when the sun sets but it's still

early, women prepare small birds,
unstuffed, bony,
and the family eats.
And then it sleeps.
One of the young boys or girls
enters a weightless dream and rises,
not in the night, but through the air.

Late

(*On lines by Elizabeth Bowen*)

It is late and the others have turned
off the lights to their rooms.
They are sleeping, or they are about to sleep,
or they are holding each other
in arms wrapped for sleep.
In the hotel only the lights of my room
call out to the solitary boats
staked to the warm bay.
What keeps me awake is indistinct.
You told me that without their indistinctness
things do not exist, you cannot desire them.
I think of you, what has not been said
and what remains unknown.
I return to claim what is unclear
as the guests of the hotel
finally release themselves to the night,
give the hotel over to its own settling in—
the natural progress of the night here.
I follow it. It becomes what is clear
as I hold both ends of dialogue,
asking my questions, answering for you.
If there were a truth in this hotel at night
it would bring me no sleep.
It makes nothing clear.
I say what comes to mind.
What comes to mind is the unsaid—
inflection your sweet device—your profile
at the window the day you turned to me to say

that those who never lie are never wholly alone.
It is late and the night air is fat with water.
I sit with you here, waiting for you to turn
again from that window and talk to me.

Return, Starting Out

There it is, the jagged sprawl of the familiar
landscape gripping the bay, urging itself
forward into the warming water of the straits
and the lean winter fish that are picking up speed.

How much the same it is! Only I turned slightly, just now,
against it—this familiar! I touch it now and everything
is slightly less known and unknown—myself,
and others, houses the same color, repainted, or not here.

Now if I reach out into the air there is no sadness
in the empty space I receive, no sadness in the wood
of the oars when I take a rented boat into the bay
and let it drift, not driven but enchanted by current and
    wind.

Sitting in this boat, I look back at the rooms of houses.
What irritable knots of light they seem from here in
    half-light,
what irresistible nests of only a little warmth, smells
of whatever meats are over the braziers.

I am not fishing in this boat, it is becalmed.
I am not thinking deeply out here, no meditation.
I am floating, moving where the wood of the boat
moves, merely floating, looking back.

Birthright

I think they go back to visit
but not to remember,
they must have made some kind of peace
and let those years move on,
but if you let go too soon
some things disappear forever
and those who live there now
will inherit your past.

Return

(FOR ELLEN)

Come back again and again, the fields no
longer hold their colors on limbs of light

over the earth, under the sky, over the soft
Dichondra, the clover and weeds that spread,

that pressed their dark root systems into the rich fields.
The old neighbors have passed quietly into the earth.

Your family has broken down and is traveling.
Still, this is where your mouth in humor first closed

over the mouth of the girl who lived behind you,
where you learned to live on the edge of talking.

Come back, the fields are gone and your friends are gone,
the girl behind you has married into another city, the roads

out of town are direct now and fast, and everyone
you knew is gone or no longer wants to know you.

But you must return, back to the long stretch of main street
reaching across the entire length of the valley,

back to the mild, midwinter days around Christmas,
back to what is now only remembered because nothing

is the same here anymore. There are no fields, nothing
edible on the land anymore—only the traffic moving

this way, then back again, then back again.
The light is no longer reflected in the earth

but you return because there is always something
that survives: come back again to old friends

living against dark fields, come back again, the family
holding dinner for you, come back, come back again.

Night Food

I talked with those who fished the Santa Monica pier at three in the morning. They waited for crabs, for stray game fish, for bottom feeders. Some used flashlights, some rusty treble hooks to snag what was there. But none of them was a fisherman. Each one had, as I remember it, his or her own calling. There was the French philosopher who had fallen in love with Kierkegaard's Cordelia, and fished to remind himself of the depths of human emotions. There was the three-hundred-pound Mexican who brought one or two live bonito and set them out into the water with ninety-pound test and wire leader, hoping for the shark that came in each morning around five, or a stray black sea bass. There was also the black woman who fished from the darkest corner of the pier. She never talked, but always caught a gunnysack full of green crabs and was gone by five. Sometimes I took friends there, but they couldn't understand its particular appeal—the fish smell of the wood, the merry-go-round, collapsed under white canvas, the live bait swimming in zinc pails—how strange it must have been to be there after a late movie and popcorn, to hear of Cordelia in the accent of the intense Frenchman in his blue turtleneck, or to watch the silent black woman pull green crabs out of the murky water. I took those young friends for french fries at the all-night diner on the fishing deck, and home. Then I returned to the pier, to resume conversation—perhaps with the bearded wino who maintained he had fished that pier ten hours a day for thirty-five years. He told me about the night the albacore and tuna swept in from deeper water and snapped the poles of everyone except the French-man, who was in the hospital having his gall bladder removed. I heard about the time the Mexican hooked a hundred-pound sea bass. With the help of the Frenchman and three tourists, he managed to coax it into the net of a local Coast Guard cadet. What a gentle community we were—once the well-dressed couples left in their tuned-up cars. For years I hardly missed a night. After work in the hospital, I changed into a sweater and jeans, gathered my equipment—for I had begun fishing after the second or third month—and took the freeway to the pier. I doubt that I caught more than ten fish the entire time I spent there—I gave the hundreds of green crabs I snagged to the black woman. What did it matter when I learned of Cordelia, whom I too soon coveted? Or watched the tired Mexican bring in tires, jungles of seaweed, and parts of outboard motors? Maybe they are still there, all of them, their poles held resolutely in the wet sea air, night fishing.

Sunday Avenue

It's Sunday again, but there will be
no calls home, no walks east in Manhattan
to the docks, or to the bakeries south
of Houston Street. Only muted sun
off the Avenue, wilted endive
for a snack and Riesling
from Oregon. Geographical,
restrained and locked here
behind the finest cylinders abstract
fear can buy: Yale and Medeco. Sunday
afternoon behind a book with Sunday
photographs of New Orleans and Europe,
or old travel diaries: Morocco
and Cairo, a 1972
New York New York. What is it
the black cat dreams of over on the sofa?
She is waiting for the spring and the spring
flies, waiting for the roof weeds
to rise up so she can again graze Sundays
when there is the terrace to sweep and pace.
In Pittsburgh my mother marinates fish
on Sunday. In Los Angeles my sisters
cover their redwood fences with redwood
stain—old blood like the light of afternoon
air here, nothing to do but hold on to
what doesn't want to leave anyway. I
am thinking of you who left on Sunday,
another Sunday, dry like this one, and
although it's Sunday again, no calls home.

The Hermit

I live at a distance,
far enough to watch them
move in the city.
I watch the couples walk.
It's quiet here, a house
of air, soundless.
I don't let others in.
At night I can see their lights,
their woodsmoke going off into the sky.
What I do is nothing.
My wife is enclosure, my children
the windows of the house.
I don't let others in.
What a good thing this is.
What a good thing it is
to sit down alone and eat,
to enter bed empty and awake,
full of what arrives, bodiless,
in sleep. The days, the days,
I don't let others in.
How friendly they seem
in their city without sound,
without texture or smell—this distance.
They could be lifeless, or something else,
they could be in love,
they could be everything
that thrives in a life with others.
It doesn't matter, this distance I keep—
I have fires, my meals, sleep
with its net that drags their streets,

invisible, hungry.
I bring it back at daylight,
I don't let others in.
The road outside my house
leads to the city
but doesn't return—
like fish scales, like hooks.
There is no reason to take that walk.
How well I know the city.
I don't let others in.
I don't let others in.
You can't leave a wife of enclosure.
You can't leave a house of air.

How to Eat Alone

While it's still light out
set the table for one:
a red linen tablecloth,
one white plate, a bowl
for the salad
and the proper silverware.
Take out a three-pound leg of lamb,
rub it with salt, pepper and cumin,
then push in two cloves
of garlic splinters.
Place it in a 325-degree oven
and set the timer for an hour.
Put freshly cut vegetables
into a pot with some herbs
and the crudest olive oil
you can find.
Heat on a low flame.
Clean the salad.
Be sure the dressing is made
with fresh dill, mustard
and the juice of hard lemons.
Open a bottle of good late harvest zinfandel
and let it breathe on the table.
Pour yourself a glass
of cold California chardonnay
and go to your study and read.
As the story unfolds
you will smell the lamb
and the vegetables.
This is the best part of the evening:

the food cooking, the armchair,
the book and bright flavor
of the chilled wine.
When the timer goes off
toss the salad
and prepare the vegetables
and the lamb. Bring them out
to the table. Light the candles
and pour the red wine
into your glass.
Before you begin to eat,
raise your glass in honor
of yourself.
The company is the best you'll ever have.

For Cats

They can take your breath away
but not from your mouth
directly. Old women
have passed this kind of thing
on—
there's almost no truth in it.

They can take your breath away
if you sleep with them sleeping
with their good fur over your mouth,
but this kind of thing happens almost
never—
cats won't stay long enough in that position.

They can take your breath away
when they are beautiful
and watchful with their affections,
if they know how to move and when
for you—
if they drop from great height without sound,

or clean themselves for hours in the sun,
or sit on your lap, their throats vibrato
against the thrumming of your fingers,
or stretch on their way out of the room, moving
perfectly—
they can take your breath away.

Insomnia

It is sometimes the easiest thing
in the world, the world
closing down, lost
to the internal light
of the psychic drama.
The eyes in disuse twitch
like the tripping frames
of a motion picture slowing
to a standstill.
We wake not entirely whole
into the darkness looking
for the light, the glass
of stale water
and a sense of place, our eyes
free to catch the real passing of time.

Lights in the Dark

They beg for the bodies of light
placed in our rooms,
pressing in against the screen
to follow the air away
from what they no longer want.
I know the forest continues on and on
toward some central darkness
where not even insects bother to go,
so airless, so still.
But here's a house in all this darkness,
each room with a light, and we sit
as the evening gets later and later.
Finally, there is only the pellucid sound
of wings on the wire meshing, our own
darkness calling forth from the distance.

Under Darkness

Nothing changes, darkness
over the body holds steady and complete,
consumes light as it lifts over the ledge
of sea and falls onto the body asleep.

In the darkness the blank pennies of death
over the lids hold eyes in darkness.
The body falls back and back,
pressed into the recessive landscapes

of sleep. No one walks here, or here, or here.
There are those spinning in spokes of light
who remain unseen. This is the literature
and history of light, light that is in air

but no longer alive at its source:
it arrives homeless and dying.
Again and again no change, setting out alive
and bright, moving forward with the dark

already eating at the base and the home wood.
The body and the body's beauty are lights
that belong in air,
leaving nothing, going nowhere, suspended

in the dark, tunneling with what life is left
through their own dark root systems.
Pennies rattle on the fluttering eyes of those still
alive, those feeding off the flesh of darkness.

The Dwelling Air

There are times when you can believe
that you live there now—

the air so pure, so personally without
gravitation, that suspension in that place

seems to be where you already reside.
Outside, the weather gets colder, then warmer,

and those you know get older, they pass their days.
Some of them stay in the same place and plant

a new lineage to pass on what they can.
Others go too far and decide not to come back—

off rivers, out of forests and cities
where they survive the fevers for a time.

Outside, events come to an end,
you understand that we are at first left with

what is most sorrowful, but even that is over
in a while, and the solitudes that do not end

begin, where suspension and the passing of time
are the same things, when you begin there for good.

The Correspondent

From the stories he told
we could put together for ourselves
a sense of the climate,
and the balance, as he saw it, between
his side and theirs. They dug in
along the hills and for weeks,
during the season of low clouds, kept watch.
His side, from their fortifications,
did about the same. They waited.
They engaged each other and moved
to new positions. Then all this
began again—
different seasons, different people.
From his stories
we came to know the one story,
as if we too had been there.
In time, they became the stories
we passed on as our own lives,
not taken from those he told us,
which we can no longer remember.

Snapshot of Hue

(FOR ROBERT STONE)

They are riding bicycles on the other side
of the Perfume River.

A few months ago the bridges were down
and there was no one on the streets.

There were the telling piles on corners,
debris that contained a little of everything.

There was nothing not under cover—
even the sky remained impenetrable

day after day. And if you were seen
on the riverbank you were knocked down.

It is clear today. The litter in the streets
has been swept away. It couldn't have been

that bad, one of us said, the river barely moving,
the bicycles barely moving, the sun posted above.

River Passage

The river town is too far now
by boat, for most,
and the forest has closed
over the only landing strip.

On the river nothing
beyond the outskirts
of the capital
makes a stranger welcome—

not even the inoculated
winter travelers so earnest
with sketch pads and pills,
ready for the darkness—

the darkness there is off
limits, the curfew begins
at sunset, is lifted
with the rising sun.

But we have come all this way,
it is the hot season along the river,
it is beginning for us.
We move through the overhang

of trees and river life, the razor
of water slicing into the dark vegetation
that one day opens onto the town
we've been awaiting for so long.

They come out to greet us as residents.
They come out to greet us as friends long lost.
They come out into the river light
to welcome us as one of their own,

and when we pass from river to land
we look again at the river
as it takes the first turn back
upriver to the capital of strangers.

This Place

There is no one left to talk here,
the talkers in their skirts and trousers
are in the field now,
the sky is pink-and-white fish-spine.

Already they are in the pass,
they are on the far shore of the lake,
they are on the farthest oak ridge,
and now they are gone and now there is nothing—

no sounds from the throats of men and women
who stay behind, nothing said.
I've been thinking about this place
where no man talks, where women

never laugh or weep or call out in the night.
How the quiet is here! Only the smoke of talkers
lifting in the half-light of their last day.
They have gone to the cities,

and they have gone on talking,
but there is no one here who speaks.
There is this hand
that holds you, it says nothing.

This is for you, that under
the diminished sun, balanced where once
the talkers passed, there is nothing left to say,
only these fingers, holding you here

into the night. Stay quiet, you who say nothing,
do you imagine you hear the last of them?
Can you see their smoke rise and fade? Now hold these hands
that with such care hold you where no one speaks.

II

Dead Fish

The pale arc of line feeds
into the green of the bank
and drops its fly into the shallows
of the stream in shadow
without sound. The line floats down
onto water and the current
takes it on, deeper.
Cast after cast the fly moves
in the afternoon
from one edge of the stream
to the other, snapped into place
as I move downstream, replacing
cast with the imagined weight
of a feeder trout unseen in current.
Shadows wobble the stream.
I see a fish hung
near the bank, gills at rest,
life only in buoyancy,
its resistance against current.
I move close, drop the fly
upstream so it floats back
over the dull eyes of the sleeper
fish. The fly floats past.
It won't move. It won't move
as I move closer. It hangs there
and won't move as I bring down the rock
with terrified force. In the explosion
of water I see the white fungus
it has grown, the sucker mouth
and its full fish-body not trout.

It is imperfection I hate,
the age, the gamelessness of immobility,
the sudden decision to live.

When it floats to me
later, having fought to free itself
from branches of the stream trees,
I need its dead weight against my leg
to know ambition and its net, how it turns
on the object pursued,
dead now and my prize
as I cast in pale light,
the evening
pulled in on a fly.

Leaving Summer

(FOR JEANNE)

So lucky here, a woodfire in autumnal
New England August, trees loosening
a redness along the greenish hills:
blood-necklace, ruby-river, vein-creeper.

All summer we've sent out flies into insect-air,
jigging over streambeds for trout, fly-drift
over pools, casting into shadows
then fading light under the White Mountains

Frost diminished in his poem "New Hampshire."
We stir the coals in the pit of coals outside
and turn the red meat, the red wine in our hands.
And we look into the tapered woods.

So dark out there, beyond the little poundings
of white moths, the net of light thrown
from the porch and moon before it grows dark
in black birch. The sounds in the woods are those

we throw ourselves to keep something mysterious,
or merely unknown. We follow the sounds
and for a moment leave what is so lucky here—
woodsmoke, end-of-the-meal—ourselves absent, looking back.

Trees in Various Climates

There is something to say
in the company of others.
Alone, there is the viewing
of the evening sky, slate
and whitewash blue, the color
of the walls in the northern towns
of Morocco, although the sky
I'm thinking of is Italian
through stripped river trees
in the last days of the year.

In New Hampshire a few friends
tried to talk all afternoon one day,
about everything that was serious
and not serious in our lives.
We went from room to room trying,
and finally outside, into the thick
summer New England birch forest
which flushed the breath of ferns
at us, but all that came of it
was the attempt to talk, and that,
like many things unfinished,
became what was important.

Today, we each look out
at the weather in the morning,
the light of late afternoon,
and hold awhile that information.

The trees of Tangier, in December,
retain more color than the trees
of Rome, which let a light
into the room that reveals
too much of the secret sleep,
where everything is portrayed
as if actually uttered
through the skeletal trees.

Calling West

(FOR BOB)

Outside, something is always budding,
and he is telling me about it.
He has been cutting wood for the fire
and he can make me smell the warm dust
of the cut western wood. I know
the fish or mushrooms are doing fine
in butter, shallots, and white wine,
low heat: the family too is well.
When he finishes the conversation
there is a little laugh to remind me
of the happiness found at last, outside
cities where something is always budding.

Between us the exchange of notes:
a gesture seen at dusk that continues
to move, something else remembered
or a few lines scratched onto a yellow pad
and preserved: what it was you thought
she said on that beach, eastern grasses,
western grasses, wildflowers, the cool
and balmy coastal evenings we note.

I seem all right tending the sawdust fire—
what's natural here?—the cat set
like a black almond before it nine
floors up. There is the steady beat
of the neighbor's jazz through the floor,
the melody not even distant through
two feet of plaster and Stanford White
construction, the drone of cars he hears

on the line, the hard sounds that explode, fade,
rise up in metallic street-air, wind down.

We have all left cities, some for other cities,
some for hills near an ocean, and many find
what they think they want living with others
after years of living with others.

We agreed on this one afternoon
on the Lower East Side of Manhattan. It was summer
and the air wouldn't move all day. Our walk
through the transplanted neighborhoods
was placed crossbeam against the long vertical
years we had each already lived.

Between us we have everything to say wherever
we find ourselves, eastcoast, westcoast,
sustaining the exaggeration of those
who remember inexactly later,
but will now talk on into the windless coastal nights.

Night Scene

(FOR BILL)

The train passes through the night,
through tunnels like the night,
through open fields, at night.
The elemental racket of the rails
through the wine country of Umbria
keeps the two of us alert but saying nothing,
the wind whistling the second-class

compartments, our train from Rome to Terontola.
We see from the corridor windows
two circles of fire in a wine field,
perfect red arcs circumscribed in the night,
burning lightly without sound.
This is a sight we both know
will mean nothing in retelling,

that the literal fire of the two
circles in the middle of the night
will be only another event, attached to nothing.
I am relating this event
far from the fact of the train ride.
The red of the flames might seem to us now
the color of local rubesco

or the deep red of Tuscan wines.
But this is something no longer important.
The train passed late in the night through
wine fields that held two perfect circles

of fire, and we two, friends and silent,
watched it pass and at the time said nothing.
It was enough.

The End of Vigil

All night I am held in the sound
of constant thunder, inverted arcs
of lightning over the hills

outside my window. There is no
chance of dreaming tonight,
the air is so heavy

that sleep is pressed from me.
The rain flushes insects
from the wall, they must feel

that same heaviness and come out
looking for relief. In the dark
I sit with the flashing light

like the lights that enter the dark
compartments of trains as they wind
through landscapes at night.

There is something in all this show
of energy that remains static,
that is still and wants only to witness

the passing night, the passing storm,
the flow of insects out of the wall,
the anger of dreams not held in sleep,

myself sitting upright in the damp bed
listening, watching the odd shadows
drift on the walls and ceiling of the room,

drift slowly, climbing away from me
for something. When I get up there is
nothing more to see in the darkness.

I walk outside.
The rain has stopped
and already the morning

sun is soaking up the messiness of night,
moving boldly into the sky,
claiming everything.

The Romance

The Beginning

They met and in their meeting they were happy. She thought of others who had charmed her with delicacy and had left, and of the darkness in their hair. She thought such thoughts that sobered her, that brought her to him. And he in return thought of others before her, their gentle words and eyes that were as white coffins, containing roots that reached deeply to hold him. She believed that he, like her, believed that they held there in that moment of their meeting something unlike the white coffins that her eyes were for him. And in a similar way, he believed that his dark hair was without darkness for her. As they stood there with his fingers unsprung in hers and hers softly outside his, they believed that this was a meeting of two good things, that he would be there for her, and she, in return, would be there for him. And so in their meeting, with her hand and his hand for the first time one in the other, there was a happiness that both believed binding.

Status Quo

The birds with tiny particles of earth fly in through the eaves. It is autumn. It is the time of sunset. It is quiet. It is the country. It is a time for slowness of thought and movement. He tells her this, and she yawns. They know, both in their minor ways, a little secret: this then is the time of slowness. The birds and weather turn black and a winter night leans for them. There is a fire and he plays his favorite piece on their new piano. She talks. He smiles. He does not listen to her. The terrible lightness of Poulenc depresses him into brandy. She seems happy knowing he is happier than he has ever been. Her irritation is without irony. It is hours later that he, with too much brandy holding him, turns to her, a small glass of white wine from the afternoon still in her hand, with a smile on his face. "The birds," she thinks. "The autumn," she thinks. She thinks, "The time of sunset, the time of slowness." When she removes his shirt it is her little secret that starts from his flesh. Terribly happy, he lays himself on top of her: the brandy. "Don't be catty," she whispers to him after he's fallen asleep.

Final Scene

"You're joking," he exclaimed. He felt immediate relief in this little burst of emotion, and yet saw that it made no impression upon her. She had been digging in her purse for the last few minutes, her arms buried in the rubbed-out leather pouch. "A child," he thought. Her hair suddenly fell into the purse alongside her arms. And she stopped for a moment and lifted from the purse a small dark pistol. He heard the hard sound of the bullet leaving the shell. He saw it stop to hang between them. She smiled as she rolled the black gloves up her long arms, and shoved her hair back over her shoulder. "Yes," he smiled. She stood and bent back down over him. Her tiny lips moved with care over his face. When she stood up for the final time, their eyes met.

Passing

Sometimes you called on those
you'd never know
to come with you in place
of those you loved,
and talked to them
and touched them
and let them close purely
for sadness, for sadness
you'd hold them,
and you'd let them go.

Elegies for Careless Love

I / *Late October, Lake Champlain*

I've been trying to write you of that night
although you have no need
to be reminded of it—you haven't forgotten
the moon held on a stick of light
over the lake, its sudden appearance in our bed
on my shoulder, on your shoulder.
We can let it pass but nothing is over
and the imprint of your feet and hands
remains in my hands. I remember now
the moon, the lake and the room
of Vermont pine—the space
of those days when all it could do
outside was rain. Forget those nights,
that place, when we were at ease
with our predilection for the removed
nagging us back
to sleep and your dream of a blue bottle
filled with an unknown scented fluid.
Now I give you a blue container—
scent-filled—with slices of paper notes,
those phrases that can't be said.

II / Woodsmoke, Vermont

The woodsmoke drifted into the car
every time we passed a house
on that road down the center of Vermont,
and each time you told me how you loved
woodsmoke. The weather was rain
and that week was like living
in the already past—everything part
of some other time:
the odor of the room in that town,
the women on Geritol who sat
all day in the lobby.

                      And all night the scent
of woodsmoke drifted to us
in our wooden bed, all night the rain
fingered the wooden shingles
above our room. What could we have said?
Below us the old women were held
in woolen blankets
and soft white inn sheets.
And there we were, holding on
to each other,
already in the process of letting go.

III / Sleeper

I held you in the front room.
When we woke the fire was nearly out
and the wine had almost
worn off.

You said you couldn't sleep
being held,
yet you slept.

I asked if we should go
into the other room,
but you said no, that you
could never go there,
that it would be the end of everything.
We went into the other room
and it was the end of nothing,
or not of anything that had started.

I think about what you said that night.
Nothing had started that wasn't always there.

You never slept before the fire,
you never went half in dream
to the other room,

and you only dreamed
that as I held you there
you slept.

IV / *Your Hands*

You've probably put on
your white sweater

and plaid skirt,
your boots and now

shake down your hair
as you enter some dining room

vague and vain and a little
lonesome for our dark

late-night dinners in the city
when you were happy with

the candlelight, the single rose,
the hand closing on yours.

Isn't it always like that for a while?
Everything stopped, held there

with only the hands in movement.
Yours must be so cold—

do they deflect snow?—
I took them in mine,

your hands that had given up
their warmth for so long.

V / No Letters

My friend, how sad you were here—
but not too sad, not enough
in league with happiness to be happy.

The house in the Midwest, is it cheerful?
In your chair with your afternoon drink
remember how you went

this way and that way, wanted
one thing
and wanted another?

The sun sets there
but continues west. Look after it.
Listen closely as the low song begins:

from the huts of the poor,
from the tract homes of the poor,
from the mansions of the poor,

oh careless love.

VI / An End

Occasionally, it was only night. I mean
you didn't come back again

and in the morning there was nothing
left unless you had carelessly left

your scent in the room.
I remember nothing more than the idea of scent.

The only thing to do in the morning
was to begin again without you,

which I have begun to do.
The nights are shorter and spring

has come, and another who takes more care
with what she cares about

than you. I will miss you.
Do not expect applause.

Nude

In one of Watteau's pencil sketches
there's a woman sleeping on her side,
partly covered, the space behind her
darkly penciled in, her right arm
reaching out, probably around someone
who has left.
What makes me think her arm
is not merely cast out
is the way Watteau sketched dampness into her hair,
the way he remembered to pencil in
the good-time cloth-bracelet on that wrist,
and the space next to her,
which he left without a mark.

Summer Constellations

They are sorry, they bring up umbrellas
from the beach below. They are paid
for this, the boys with their deep tans
who are beautiful but feel nothing
of what is felt by some for them.
Some days it rains and the beach
is left pocked and cold.
The umbrellas are left inside.

Maybe everything here is temporary.
The couple, when the sun is out,
carry their own umbrellas
down to a few feet from the waterline.
They talk and like everyone
have their own language—the color
of their suits, the quantity
of food they bring,
the amount of chilled Chablis.

Each day, on its own, is quiet with little
detail bothering anyone. The man speaks well
with the boys, and the woman
is clever and alive with her eyes and mouth.

Sometimes the couple talk quietly together
for hours, abstractedly. They look out beyond
the line of water that dissolves at sunset,
the sun a plug that frees the water—
the water and configurations of fish
fill the sky. It is covered in discussion

as the couple walk under the kelp constellations
of evenings by the sea and continue
their amused talk, some little salt on their tongues,
the sea giving, the sea taking back,
again and again and finally,
long after the couple fall asleep
to the predictable rhythm of the tides,
the sea withdraws and the dawn sky clears.

The boys who bring up the umbrellas are sorry
because everything is temporary: the sun,
the weather, the bathers, the season, and,
although they don't know it yet and may never,
the two who walk into the water, hand in hand.

Driving

Sometimes your own past is anyone's
but yours, and you find yourself driving
through afternoons of summer heat
that are without time.
Sometimes when I think about it
we are driving along a river
with so little to say that we say nothing,
and everything that is possible to desire
passes on the river,
fighting the current back
to that place we started from.

The Storm

The Italian police stopped us today
as I passed a tiny Fiat on the road
from Perugia to Umbertide.

They were behind a few cypress trees
and I couldn't see them in my hurry
to beat home the storm over Firenze.

They told me I passed over an unbroken line,
although, standing there, I did find a small space
near where we stood and tried to make my case,

but we all smiled—the Italian workmen
had run out of paint that day, it was their mistake
although I would have passed anyway

and the two thousand lire it cost me
can't buy decent pasta anymore. The air
was stopped and it darkened over Tuscany.

We drove on into the storm and beat it home
as I knew we would, past the guinea fowl
and geese in our village of Polgeto,

and soon the rain began to fall, large drops
at first raising the dust, then gluing it down,
then filling the water tanks of Umbria.

The peasants sitting outside Polgeto's shops
stopped talking awhile, and the tree insects
too stopped their chirrs, as if to acknowledge

the storm. And then they started up again.
I awaited this beginning—nothing
is plain when heard again after silence.

I wanted to say more, how a storm registers
on the stony faces of the men outside
the *alimentari*, the insects' shutdown.

What will survive, remembering all this,
is something else—not the police or the rain
or the skies building up over the north,

but how out of the daily incidents
we find the distance not too long to go,
that we can go that distance, and continue on.

The Last Days of the Year

Sometimes the days must
  fly by
    as they say,

one year palms
  inhabited by wind and rain,
    the wet smell of wool

in the Berber markets,
  the next our room
    on Isola Tiberina

off the little Piazza
  San Bartolomeo, river-damp
    with the river patrol

at the point, waiting
  to drag out the suicides
    and driftwood.

Above Italy
  the skyline is cypress,
    black imago pressed

against the pale mauve
  of Roman winter sunset.
    You're out looking

for something in the shops
  off the Corso and I'm sitting over
    the Tiber, remembering that

one night last year
   I went deep into the markets
      of Marrakesh to find

the little birds
   made from the green
      malachite of the Atlas.

You must have sat like this
   over your mint tea thinking
      about other years

at home, your mother
   and her mother baking together
      and cleaning the silver

with the special paste
   that is one of the
      remembered decorations;

you must have thought
   I'd been gone a long time,
      waiting as it got later,

as I wait now
   for you, the same sounds
      of the cars outside, passing by.

This Time of the Year

I've stayed awhile along the river
that runs through the city, walked
upriver to the monuments north of our rooms,
and downriver, over to the city center
to look at the store windows and walking couples

and the Caravaggios in San Luigi dei Francesi.
The sky has cleared itself of the end of the year.
It is almost warm, the burning of oxygen
by the crowds in the large decorative piazzas,
the unobstructed sun in these windless streets.

It is the time of day when the bells begin
and the trattorias open their doors onto tables
of cold dishes floating in olive oil.
I stayed awake last night to consider yet again
the old meditation—in this city of what has remained

my panic is a soft commotion, but I am closer to it.
The automobiles that gun the streets brush by me,
and above, the plaster gods and goddesses carry on,
the air so pure, so warm for this time of year,
and so permanent.

Spend

Diminishing returns she said,
you've got to make up your mind someday—
good money after bad my father would have added
had he thought about it, and he did.
He didn't talk much period, his pursuits
being bargains, discounts, the model
that looked like the real thing but never was.
I told my friends he worked in the metal business—
they thought I said meadow business,
but asked no questions and I didn't correct them.
He died too early to understand someone else
and I grew up too slowly to help him out.
After these ten years it doesn't matter anymore
because I can understand it all. What comes back
is not what you've given, that much we know
no matter how slowly we've grown into the world.

But you have to decide someday, this way or that,
to toss the good after the bad or whatever it is
you have to give. I have the usual memories,
the collective sadness of growing up among the dying,
never knowing to say enough at the right time—
I am my father's son, but I've learned to spend
with a carelessness that would have won me nothing
in my father's eyes, they were so pale blue.
Living well doesn't cost much if style
is what you're after. My friends can all have
the best of what they want, but their wants
are simple and elegant. My father wanted so little

that it cost him everything, with nothing coming back.
But he would have said that if you wait long enough
something will come back. Diminishing returns.
Nothing that needs to come back comes back.

Portoncini dei Morti

In the *Analects* Confucius says,
The way out is via that door. How is it
that nobody recognizes this method?

In Gubbio, an Umbrian city
the most purely medieval in Italy, the buildings
have what the Italians call *portoncini dei morti,*
the little doorways of the dead.
When the dead of the family went through the door
for the last time they plastered it up.

It wasn't for the dead they did this,
but for themselves—they knew
death was the last farewell,
plastered or not, remembered or not.

Confucius was wrong, wasn't he? A door
is not the simplest solution.
I'm thinking about history and the departure
of the loved, about fathers
or men who raised sons they couldn't know.

I'm talking to those who have no ghost doorway
to mark their leaving us, who were carried
to the place that takes care of lost love—
in our country people die away from home,
it's part of the economy,
and the economy of loving.

The medieval Italians knew something
about dying and about love,
they closed the door for the dead.
What do the dead open for us
but the door that opens onto what there was?
What do we do for the dead but lower them
into the earth, shovel earth over
their eyes, and this, like the plaster
of the Italians, keeps the living out of
the way of those dead we have lost.

Intelligence is not needed to find a door
after death in the presence of love,
nor are doors answers to anything
that hides some part of ourselves.
The question is how to turn back—
the Italians were right: let the dead
leave us unattended and unencumbered.
Let us build new doors that the family
may leave together. This is the solution
and Confucius too was right,
that we will find new ways of being together
among the living.

Notes

"*Late*" / Lines in this poem are taken from Elizabeth Bowen's novel *The House in Paris*.

"*Return*" / Dichondra is a cloverlike grass grown in southern California.

"*Snapshot of Hue*" / was inspired by a passage from Michael Herr's book *Dispatches*.

Daniel Halpern was born in Syracuse, New York, in 1945, and grew up in Los Angeles and Seattle. He earned degrees from California State University at Northridge and Columbia University, and for two years lived in Tangier, Morocco, where he started the literary magazine *Antaeus,* which he still edits. Poems, translations, fiction, and articles by him have appeared in *The New Yorker, The Atlantic Monthly, The New York Review of Books, Harper's, The New Republic,* and many other publications. He formerly taught at The New School for Social Research and at Princeton University, and he is now chairman of the Graduate Writing Division of Columbia University.